Operation Dump the Boyfriend

by Sherry Shahan
illustrated by Estella Hickman

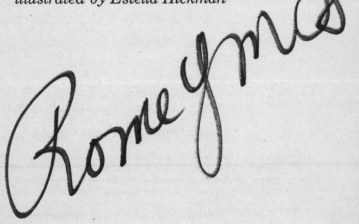

Published by Willowisp Press, Inc.
401 E. Wilson Bridge Road, Worthington, Ohio 43085

Printed in the United States of America

10 9 8 7 6 5 4 3 2 1

ISBN 0-87406-287-X

To Tina, a kindred spirit, heart and soul

One

"MACARONI and cheese, again?" Cindy Brunner said with disgust in her voice. "Mom, tell me I'm hallucinating! I'm the only kid in the whole school who has macaroni and cheese three times a week. We have it so often, my blood is probably turning to cheese!"

Cindy was leaning over the pot on the stove with her nose wrinkled in distaste. Her mother was at the sink with her elbows deep in dishwashing suds.

"Now Cindy," her mother said while scrubbing a pan. "We don't have it that often. And you know that I'm in a hurry tonight. Tomorrow night we'll have something different. Maybe a nice healthy omelette with mushrooms and green peppers."

Cindy groaned. An omelette was about as bad as macaroni and cheese. Cindy longed for the days before her parents split up. Back then they'd had fancy dinners every night. Sometimes they'd have pot roast or fried chicken. Now, with all her mom's classes at the university, she was too busy to fix any of her specialties. And when she did have time to cook, she was always making something low calorie and healthy. It might be good stuff for moms, but not for kids at all. At least Cindy didn't think so.

Cindy knew why her mom was in a hurry. And why she'd been on a diet and a nervous wreck all week. Tonight was her big date with some guy. It would be the first time she'd gone out with anyone except for Cindy's dad since before they'd been married. And Cindy wasn't too happy about it!

"Where's Mr. What's-his-name taking you?" Cindy asked her mother.

"His name is Joe Wattle and we're going out to dinner."

"Mom, do you know what a wattle is?" Cindy asked with a grin.

Her mom shook her head.

"A wattle is the skin that hangs from the neck of a turkey. It was one of our bonus vocabulary words." Cindy tried to keep a straight face. "Mom, you really can't go out with a guy whose name is Wattle. I mean, suppose you got married? Then you'd be Mrs. Wattle—with little Wattle kids!"

"Cindy, this is our first date," her mother said calmly. "And we're only going out to dinner."

Cindy stomped her feet on the floor. "How can you go out to dinner when we're stuck with macaroni and cheese!"

"Maybe I'll bring you a doggie bag," Mrs. Brunner said brightly.

Cindy had spent a lot of time thinking about her mother's eating habits. She decided that the reason her mom made macaroni and cheese was because then she wouldn't be tempted to eat it. Back in the days when they had steak and baked potatoes, her mom would pig out on butter, sour cream, and bacon bits. Now her mother wrote down everything she ate in a journal.

"If I don't watch my figure, no one else will!" Cindy remembered her mother saying.

Cindy didn't think anyone should watch her mother's figure, except of course, for her father.

Cindy had a journal, too. Every time Paul McCloskey said something to her, she wrote it down. One day she wrote, "Paul McCloskey called me Bozo the Clown today." She didn't even mind when he teased her about her red frizzy hair. Her grandmother had told her that boys only teased you when they liked you.

And Cindy really liked Paul McCloskey. Everything about him was neat—from his button-down shirt to his patterned socks to the briefcase he carried to school! Well, it wasn't a briefcase exactly, it was more like a cloth satchel. It was just like the one her father had carried to work every day when he had lived with them.

Cindy's thoughts were interrupted when her kid sister, Karen, ran into the kitchen. "Zoom ba-room!" she roared. Her arms were stretched out like two airplane propellers. "Guess what I am?"

"A helicopter?" Cindy asked.

Karen shook her head. "No!"

Mrs. Brunner tried. "A choo-choo train?"

Karen scrunched her mouth and repeated her imitation of an engine. "Va-room! Va-room! I'm a motormouth!"

Mrs. Brunner smiled. "Where did you learn that?"

"At preschool," Karen answered. "My teacher calls all the kids motormouths."

Cindy lifted Karen onto her booster chair with a laugh. "Now it's your turn to guess," Cindy said. "What are we having for dinner?"

Karen's blue eyes widened. "Chocolate chip cookies?"

"Nope." Cindy looked at Karen, grinning. "We're having big orange worms."

"You can't fool me," Karen said. "Worms don't come in orange flavors."

"You're right," Cindy said. "They're really a special kind of shoelace with cheese."

Karen lifted her foot and studied the laces on her shoes. "Yuck!"

Mrs. Brunner took a salad bowl out of the refrigerator and served the salad onto plates. Then she dished up the macaroni and cheese and added a couple of crackers to each plate. "What would you like to drink?" she asked the girls.

Karen smacked her lips. "Catsup!"

Her mom looked surprised. "You want to drink catsup?"

Cindy laughed. "With or without a straw?"

"No, Sissy! I want catsup on my shoelaces!"

"I bet you'd put catsup on ice cream if we'd let you," Cindy said.

"Ummmmmm!" Karen agreed. "Catsup on ice cream!"

Her mom set down Karen's and Cindy's plates. "It's getting late," she said, fluffing Karen's fine blond curls. "I'd better start getting ready."

Cindy glanced at the clock. Her mom's date wasn't due to arrive for a half hour. That would be just enough time for her to try on everything in her closet. Then she'd probably end up wearing what she decided to wear two weeks ago when he first asked her out—designer blue jeans and an oversized hand-knit sweater.

"God is great. God is good." Cindy said, clasping her hands and bowing her head. "Let us thank him for our food—even if it is macaroni and cheese. Amen."

Half of the noodles on Cindy's plate stuck to the roof of her mouth when she began to eat. It took several heaping gulps of milk to wash them down. She piled the other half of her noodles on Karen's plate. It was the only way to make sure there weren't any macaroni and cheese leftovers. Otherwise, they'd have macaroni and cheese all weekend.

"More catsup?" Cindy asked.

Karen nodded. "*Catsup!*"

Cindy gave Karen some more catsup and then went to check on her mother. Mrs. Brunner was the type who got flustered under pressure. During finals week last quarter, she was an absolute basket case. Even though Cindy wasn't happy about her mom entering the dating world, she didn't want her making a fool of herself.

Cindy dove stomach-first on her mom's bed. "You didn't spray your armpits with hair spray like you did before finals, did you?" she asked.

Her mom shook out her designer jeans. "Aren't you ever going to let me live that down?"

Cindy giggled. "I hope your date appreciates it that you lived on celery sticks and protein shakes for a week so you could fit in those jeans."

Cindy's mom scooted into her jeans with a grunt. "I hope you're not planning on giving away any of my secrets."

"And ruin your chances? Not me!"

With her jeans zipped and buttoned, Mrs. Brunner sat down on the edge of the bed. "How do you know so much about dating, Cindy?

You're not still watching soap operas after school, are you?"

"I can't help it," Cindy said. "I'm hooked. Besides, how else am I suppose to learn about life?"

Her mom gave her a serious look and Cindy knew it was time to change the subject. Just then the doorbell rang.

Mrs. Brunner looked nervous and checked herself in the mirror.

"Darn, I forgot my earrings," Mrs. Brunner said. "Cindy, would you mind answering the door?" she asked.

Cindy didn't want to answer the door. She didn't want to invite Mr. Wattle into the living room. She didn't want her mom going out on a date. Somehow, it just didn't seem right.

"Do I have to?" Cindy whined.

Two

CINDY pressed her nose against the living room window. She watched as Mr. Wattle opened the car door for her mother. Karen stood on her tiptoes and held onto the windowsill.

"Where's Mommy going?" Karen asked.

Cindy made a face. It was awful having to watch your mother go out on a date. "She's going to dinner with Mr. Wattle," she said, watching as the car backed down the driveway.

Karen took a lint-covered cookie from her pocket and stuffed it in her mouth. She chewed solemnly. "Is she going to come back?"

"Of course she's coming back," Cindy snapped. "What a stupid question!"

"Daddy didn't come back." Karen's tone was very matter-of-fact.

It was questions like these that made Cindy wish she were an only child. "What're you talking about?" she asked. "We saw Daddy last weekend. We went to the movies and you threw popcorn at the lady in front of us, remember?"

"Yeah, that was fun," Karen giggled, and then turned serious. "Why doesn't Daddy live here anymore?"

"Because," Cindy said.

"Because why?" Karen asked impatiently.

"Just because," Cindy said in exasperation. "That's why."

Cindy didn't understand why her parents got a divorce. Her mother said she still loved her father in her own way. Her father said he still loved her mother in his own way. And they both said they still loved her and Karen. Did that make sense? Cindy didn't think so.

"This is going to be the longest night of my life," Cindy sighed.

Karen took her soggy thumb out of her mouth. "I want to watch TV!"

"It's bedtime," Cindy said.

Cindy lifted Karen to her hip and they walked down the hall. Bright yellow wallpaper with teddy bears decorated Karen's bedroom. Her toy box matched her wallpaper, but most of her toys were scattered on the floor.

"Sleep tight and don't let the bedbugs bite," Cindy said as the telephone rang.

Cindy hurried down the hall to the kitchen extension. "Hello?" she answered.

"Muffin? Is that you?" her grandmother's voice asked.

"Nana!" Cindy said. "I'm so glad it's you!"

Boy, was that the truth! Nana was her best friend in the whole world, at least in the grown-up world. Her mom was her friend, too. But a mom was always a mom.

"Is something wrong?" Nana asked.

"You can say that again!" Cindy made herself comfortable on the floor, settling in for a long

conversation. She untied her shoes and kicked them off. "Do you know what Mom is doing this very minute?"

"Is this a game?" Nana asked.

"I wish it were a game," Cindy said. "I don't want you to be shocked, Nana, but Mom went out on a date."

"I'm sorry, Muffin," Cindy's grandmother said in an understanding tone. "But you knew it was bound to happen sooner or later."

"But, Nana, wait'll I tell you what a turkey this guy is. You won't believe it. First, he patted me on top of my head, like I was a dog or something. And that's not the worst part. Every time he said something to Karen, he screeched in a high-pitched voice. He sounded like Donald Duck or something. Besides, what if Daddy finds out? It might ruin their chances of getting back together."

"There's not much chance of that, Muffin. The divorce has been final for several months."

"Well, this Mr. Wattle better not think he's

going to move in or anything like that."

"I don't think you have anything to worry about. This is only their first date," Cindy's grandmother said with a laugh.

Her laugh was like a bathtub of warm bubbles. It made Cindy feel good all over. "Yeah, I guess you're right. I love you, Nana."

After Cindy hung up from talking with her grandmother, she decided to call her friend Tina. She and Tina had been best friends since kindergarten. Every year, along with their friend Beth, they formed a secret club and did all kinds of crazy things.

This year's first meeting of the secret club was Monday. She and Tina had a lot to plan—initiations, elections, all kinds of things. But Cindy didn't want to talk to Tina about the club. She wanted to talk to Tina about her mom. Tina's mom and dad had been divorced for six years and Tina was always talking about her mom's boyfriends. Cindy learned a lot about that junk from soap operas. But tonight she wanted to talk to someone with firsthand experience.

Tina picked up the phone on the first ring. Cindy was glad. Tina had a little sister named Lindsey, who was just a year older than Karen. If Lindsey had answered the phone, Cindy would have to talk to her about teddy bears and cartoons for half an hour before even getting Tina on the phone.

"You'll never guess what happened!" Cindy blurted out to Tina without even saying hello.

"Yeah I saw it, too," Tina said in a rush. "Can you believe it? On the soaps this afternoon, April put an ad in the personal column of the newspaper for a date. I guess anyone can put an ad in the paper to advertise for a date. I'd advertise for a blond surfer with blue eyes." Tina stopped for just a second and sighed. "Remember the lifeguard at the beach last year? The one with the curly chest hair? Maybe he'd answer my ad."

"I wasn't talking about the soap opera."

"What's the matter with you?" Tina asked. "I

thought you'd be excited! If April starts dating the guy from the ad—whoever it turns out to be—then her engagement with Jeff would be off. I never did like Jeff, did you?"

Cindy wrapped the telephone cord around her finger. "How can I get excited over a dumb soap opera when my whole life is falling apart?"

"What're you talking about?" Tina asked curiously.

Cindy fidgeted uneasily. "Mom had a date tonight," she finally said.

"Wow!" Tina said excited. "Start from the very beginning. I want to know *everything*."

Cindy leaned back and tapped her foot against the kitchen wall. "That's it," she said. "There's nothing else to tell."

"What do you mean there's nothing else to tell? What's his name? What kind of a car does he drive? Where does he work? How much money does he make? Where does he—"

"Hold it!" Cindy cut her off. "How am I suppose to know all of that? I just met the guy."

"Well, it wouldn't hurt if your mom married someone rich, would it?"

"I don't want her marrying anyone," Cindy said, annoyed. Except Dad, she thought to herself.

"If you think this guy's bad, you should see the guy my mom's dating," Tina said.

Tina spent the next fifteen minutes describing her mom's dates. She had even developed a point system for rating them as possible stepfathers. The guy who drove a flashy sportscar received a five-point bonus. The guy who worked at a fitness center had five points deducted, because his biceps bulged through his shirt sleeves. Tina thought muscles were disgusting.

But the whole time that Tina was talking, Cindy was thinking about the soap opera Tina had described. An idea was starting to form in Cindy's mind. "Anyone can take out a personal ad to advertise for a date . . ." Tina had said earlier. And if anyone could do it, she could. She could advertise for a date for her mom. In fact, she could line up a lot of dates for her mom. That way, her mom would forget about Mr. Wattle. And she'd be dating so many men that she wouldn't be able to get serious with just one of them. Her mom might even decide that her dad was better than all of them. It just might work.

"Cindy, are you listening to me?" Tina's voice cracked through the receiver."

"Uh, Tina, I was just thinking about something. About that personal ad . . ."

"Yeah, what about it? I thought you didn't want to talk about soap operas."

"This is different. How did April do it? I mean, how does this personal ad thing work?"

"April put an ad in the paper that described herself and the kind of guy she wanted to meet. The ad didn't have her name on it or anything, just a number."

"A number. What for?" Cindy asked.

"Well, if a guy likes her ad, he can take an ad out that responds to her ad. The newspaper assigns April's ad a number so that the guy can be sure to answer the right person's ad."

"But how do they actually get together?"

"Well, if the girl wants to meet the guy in the ad, she takes out another ad and uses that guy's number. The ad would tell the guy where to meet the girl."

"Hmmm," Cindy said, the wheels of her mind in motion. "So names are never mentioned in the ad?"

"Right," Tina replied. "Not until the two people—Hey, are you thinking about what I'm thinking?"

Cindy just smiled. "I think I've got the perfect way to get my mom away from that turkey," she said happily.

Three

CINDY yawned loudly as she dragged her backpack down the hall. This was going to be a busy week. She had her secret club meeting this morning. *And* she had to get the personal ad plan into action before her mom had many more dates with Mr. Wattle.

Mrs. Brunner was standing at the stove cooking eggs. She was wearing what she usually wore to the university: jeans and a sweatshirt.

"Would you like an omelet?" her mom asked. "Or, I can scramble them for you."

The only way Cindy liked eggs was soft-boiled and put on top of a potato that had been cut open and cooked in the microwave. It was a good thing her mom had brought her leftover steak from her date. "No, thanks," Cindy said. She opened the refrigerator. "I think I'll have a cup of hot chocolate and part of that steak."

Cindy filled a cup with milk and popped it into the microwave. Then she went to the pantry for a packet of hot chocolate and a few marshmallows. She put the leftover steak on the cutting board, dividing it into three equal pieces. She'd have steak and hot chocolate for breakfast, a steak and dill pickle sandwich for lunch, and steak and *anything* for dinner.

"How'd you sleep?" her mom asked.

"Okay, I guess." But Cindy hadn't slept well at all. She'd peeked out her window and had seen her mom kiss Mr. Wattle goodnight on the front steps. It was only a kiss on the cheek, but it was a kiss all the same.

But Cindy didn't want to think about Mr. Wattle, especially while she was eating steak.

Ka-plunk. The morning newspaper hit the front door. Paul McCloskey was Cindy's paperboy and she wanted to talk him into giving her an extra paper this morning. That way she could study the personal ad section and figure out how the whole thing worked. Cindy slurped the last marshmallow out of her cup, grabbed her sandwich and backpack, and raced out of the house.

"Bye," she hollered over her shoulder.

"Have a nice day," her mom yelled behind her.

Cindy bounced down the front steps. "Hey, Paul! Wait up!"

Paul jammed his pedals backward and laid a patch of burned rubber on the sidewalk. His front tire popped off the ground, causing him to spin. The canvas bag holding the *Templeton Gazette* flew off his handlebars. More than half of the newspapers landed in a puddle in the gutter.

"I'm sorry," Cindy said.

Paul set his bike on its side and picked up one of the wet papers. Then he rubbed the water off on his corduroy pants. "Boy, am I going to get it if Mr. Kramer finds out about this."

"He won't find out," Cindy offered. "All we

have to do is rewrap the papers so the wet page is on the inside."

Paul smiled. "That's brilliant!"

Cindy blushed.

Cindy helped Paul reroll the papers. She thought the two of them made a great team, but she didn't say it out loud.

Cindy remembered the last time they made a great team. It was the first week of school and Paul picked her to play on his soccer team. She wasn't sure if he'd picked her because he liked her, or if he picked her because the gym teacher forced him to choose a girl.

When all the newspapers were rolled dry side out, Cindy helped fill the canvas bag. Then Paul swung a leg over the seat of his bike. "Climb on," he said. "I'll finish my route and then I'll give you a lift to school."

Cindy stared at the seat on Paul's bike. She didn't have to measure her rump to realize it would be tough for the two of them to fit on the seat. And her arms weren't long enough to reach the handlebars. What was she supposed to hold onto?

Cindy tightened the straps on her backpack. Instead of climbing on the seat behind Paul, she sat on the narrow bumper and steadied her tennis shoes on the frame. She eyed the springs under the seat and took hold.

Paul handed Cindy newspaper after newspaper as he pedaled his route. One paper hit Mr. Mayer's welcome mat. "Bull's-eye!" Paul yelled. Another paper missed the porch and landed in a flower bed. "I miss that one all the time, too," Paul said.

It made Cindy feel good that Paul didn't get mad over the missed porch. And when she asked if she could have one of the papers, Paul said sure. She hoped it meant that he liked her— really liked her.

Paul popped his front tire up and over the curb bordering the school, and Cindy slid off the back of the bike. "Thanks for the lift," she said.

Paul pushed his bike into the bike rack. "See

you around," he said, waving.

"Yeah, see you!" Cindy called.

Tina and Beth were waiting for Cindy at their meeting place in the last stall of the girls' bathroom. That stall wasn't used because the door was missing.

Tina pointed to her watch. "I thought we were supposed to meet at seven forty-five."

"I got hung up," Cindy answered. She didn't want to explain to Tina about Paul. Tina thought he was a nerd. "But I brought this!" she said waving the paper. "Beth, we've got this great idea for getting my mom a date. It's a perfect project for the club."

Beth's face went sour. "There's no time," she said as she ripped a piece of notebook paper into thirds and passed them out. "Write your pick for president. Then chairman of the board and secretary."

What's with her? Cindy thought to herself. If this had been fifth grade, Cindy would have written Beth's name for president. They were almost

best friends then. But something happened to Cindy and Beth's friendship when Cindy's parents split up. Beth had become distant. And Tina had become more friendly. Tina thought that divorce added a new dimension to Cindy's and her own ho-hum lifestyles.

Tina and Beth were different in other ways, too. Beth's hair was so dark that it looked like hot fudge. It was cut in a shoulder-length bob, and no matter how sweaty and hot she got during gym class, her hair always fell into place. Tina's hair, on the other hand, was the color of vanilla ice cream. It was thin and wispy. Tina was always pulling on it to make it grow longer. Cindy's own hair was reddish brown and curly. When it was humid, her short ringlets turned to frizz. Cindy thought that it made her look like Bozo the Clown.

Tina took everyone's ballots and stuffed them into the empty toilet paper dispenser. Then she poked a straightened paper clip into the dispenser and fished out a ballot.

"Who wants to open the first one?" she asked, then unfolded it herself. "Tina for president, Beth for chairman of the board—" she turned to Cindy. "Sorry."

"That's only one ballot," Beth said. She took the paper clip from Tina and hooked the remaining ballots, handing one to Cindy.

Cindy unfolded the piece of paper and immediately recognized her own handwriting. "Cindy for president," she said. "Beth for chairman of the board, and Tina for secretary."

Beth read hers, giggling. "This one says Beth for president—"

"I can't believe you guys," Tina fumed. "You voted for yourselves!"

"So did you," Cindy pointed out.

"That's different," she said. "I'm qualified."

The five-minute bell rang, and the girls picked up their backpacks. They didn't want to be late for class. Cindy led the way across the soccer field to the row of classrooms that stood on the other side of the basketball court.

"Since it was a three-way tie," Cindy began. "Why don't we have rotating terms?"

"That's a good idea," Beth agreed.

Tina marched up the steps to the door marked "Mrs. Krantz's sixth grade." Most of the kids were already in their seats. Mrs. Krantz was standing at the blackboard writing the week's spelling words in white chalk. She noticed the girls standing in the doorway.

"You'd better take your seats, girls," she said to the trio. "You don't want to be late."

Paul was standing inside the doorway taking stubby pencils out of his briefcase. "Do you want to help me deliver the papers tomorrow morning?" he asked, then cranked the pencil sharpener.

Tina turned to Cindy. "That nerd isn't talking to you, is he?"

Four

THE meeting of the secret club resumed on the walk home from school. Beth was rambling on about initiations. Last year, their initiation had been to remove the foam from the cushions in the teachers' lounge. It was Tina's idea to replace the cushions with water balloons. Cindy and Beth were against the plan. Instead, they voted to fill the cushions with large bags of potato chips.

The girls had huddled outside the teachers' lounge and waited for the sound of the crunch when someone sat down. They heard the crunch sound all right. And right after that they heard the sound of the principal's voice behind them.

They had to stay in for a whole week of recesses afterward.

"I know," Beth was saying. "How about adding black dye to the soap dispensers in the boys' bathroom?"

"I've got a better idea," Tina said, kicking a rock in front of her as she walked along. "Let's let the air out of Mr. Wattle's tires the next time he has a date with Cindy's mom. Then he'll be out of the way and we can get going on that personal ad."

"You're not going to start that again are you?" Beth sniffed. "That's all you guys ever talk about." Beth set her shoulders in a rigid pose and stomped off down the street to her house.

"What's her problem?" Tina asked.

"You got me," Cindy answered with a shrug. "She was acting weird this morning, too. Anyway, we've got to get going on this ad—before my mom has another date with Mr. Wattle."

"Call me in fifteen minutes," Tina said, as she scurried up the walk to her house.

Cindy and Tina spent the rest of the afternoon on the telephone composing ads for the personal column of the *Templeton Gazette*. The ads cost fifty cents an inch. It was a good thing Cindy still had the five dollars that her grandmother had given her for her birthday.

"How about this one?" Tina was saying. " 'Attractive older woman with hard-working children wishes to meet a man who drives a Mercedes Benz or Rolls Royce. Convertible preferred. TURKEYS NEED NOT APPLY.' "

"I like the turkey part," Cindy said, boosting herself up on the counter in the kitchen. "But Mom's not exactly older. She's only thirty-three. And if she got a guy with a Mercedes Benz, it might make Dad look bad." And the whole point, Cindy said to herself, is to get Mom back together with Dad.

Cindy studied the pad of paper in front of her. "How about 'Middle-aged woman with great personality and two well-mannered children wishes to meet middle-aged gentleman who likes to cook

gourmet meals, especially steak.' "

"Are you crazy?" Tina yelled into the receiver. "You can't put 'woman with great personality' in the ad."

"Why not?" Cindy asked, twisting the cord around her fingers. "What's wrong with my mom's personality?"

"Think about it, Cindy." Tina said. "If someone said your blind date had a great personality, what would you think?"

"I'd think he was a real dog," Cindy answered.

"Don't you think we should add something about his looks? You don't want a nerd hanging around your house. We could advertise for someone who's tall, dark, and handsome. Or would you rather have a blond lifeguard type?"

Cindy chewed on the end of her pencil. "I don't care what he looks like," she said. "As long as he's nice to Mom."

"You'd better care," Tina warned. "If you don't want to end up with a weird little half-brother or half-sister. Weirdness is carried in the genes."

"What is it with you, Tina? You're always talking about my mom getting married—and now you're talking about her having another baby." Cindy shuddered. She didn't know if she could take another kid like Karen. "Can't we take one step at a time?"

The girls spent another half hour writing and rewriting the ad. Finally, they had what they thought was a good one.

"Here goes," Tina said as she prepared to read the final draft. "I hope this is it. I'm getting writer's cramp. 'Attractive woman with promising career in psychology wishes to meet kind gentleman who likes kids. TURKEYS NEED NOT APPLY.' "

"Sounds good," Cindy said. "And how can I place the ad? Karen's always hanging around and she's sure to overhear and blab it to Mom. And where are we going to have them meet?"

"Hold on," Tina said. "One question at a time. First of all, I'll place the ad. I can use the phone in my mom's room and Lindsey will never hear."

"And what about arranging the meeting? I don't want mom to know until the last minute. She might get mad at me for interfering, but if the guy's neat enough . . . " Cindy paused and thought to herself, *but not too neat to make Dad look bad,* "she'll get over it quicker."

"Look," Tina said. "First let's just get some answers to the ad. Then we'll figure everything else out."

"Okay," Cindy said slowly. "And Tina?"

"What?" Tina answered.

"Thanks," Cindy said and hung up the phone.

Five

"WE got two replies," Tina said to Cindy as she walked through Cindy's front door on Friday evening. She held the newspaper up for Cindy to see.

The week had dragged on and on. There hadn't been any club meetings because Beth had been home sick all week. And it was just as well. That way Tina and Cindy had been able to talk about the ad without Beth getting miffed. And they had needed to talk about it, too. Mr. Wattle had called her mom twice that week. They needed to get their plans nailed down—and fast.

"Hurry up," Cindy said, as she ushered Tina upstairs to her room. "Mom and Karen will be back with the pizza any minute!"

Cindy closed her door with a bang and the two girls settled themselves cross-legged on the carpet. They opened the newspaper on the floor in front of them.

"I guess I should read what the ads say," Cindy said in a voice that wasn't quite steady.

Cindy flipped through the classified section until she spotted the heading *Personal Ads*. She scanned the column, finally locating 0110, the coded numbers corresponding to their ad.

" 'Quiet, kind gentleman,' " she read, " 'wishes to meet attractive woman with promising career in psychology.' "

"That's a boring one," Tina said. "All he did was repeat what we said in our ad."

"He doesn't sound boring to me," Cindy said. Then she read the next one. " 'Good-looking, fun-loving guy wishes to wine and dine ad number 0110. How about it?' " Cindy looked up from the paper. "I don't like the sound of this guy."

Tina cracked her gum loudly. "What are you

45

talking about?" she asked. "This one is great! Believe me, I can tell."

This time, Cindy was firm. "Forget it." She folded the newspaper, stuck it under her arm, and stood up. "It's my mother. And I like the quiet, kind gentleman."

"Girls! Pizza's on," Cindy's mother called from downstairs. Cindy had wanted to figure out how to arrange the meeting between the kind gentleman and her mother before her mother and Karen got home. But if they didn't come running in for pizza, her mother was sure to be suspicious.

"Coming," Tina and Cindy said in unison and scampered down to the kitchen.

"One half is vegetarian and the other half is pepperoni."

"I'll take a piece of pepperoni. What is that stuff on the vegetarian side anyway?" Tina asked.

"Oh, there are artichokes, peppers, and mushrooms," Mrs. Brunner said with a smile.

Tina and Cindy made a face at each other.

"Just be glad they don't put macaroni and cheese on pizza," Cindy said giggling.

"May I have some catsup?" Karen asked from her booster chair. She was piling pepperoni in one corner of her tray.

"What for?" Cindy asked. "You already have pizza sauce dripping off your chin."

Karen crossed her eyes, trying to see her chin.

Tina laughed. "Karen, you're so cute."

Cindy put a third piece of pizza on her paper plate. "Maybe we should trade sisters. If you wouldn't mind being called *Sissy*. I don't know why she can't call me Cindy like everyone else."

"She started calling you Sissy because she couldn't pronounce Cindy," her mom explained. "And the name stuck. It's the same reason you call Nana *Nana* instead of Grandma. Besides, I think Sissy is sort of cute."

Cindy rolled her eyes.

Tina turned to Mrs. Brunner. "Yesterday, my kid sister squeezed an entire tube of toothpaste in the bathroom sink. Then she smeared it in her hair! It was such a mess to clean up."

"Did I tell you about the time Karen escaped from the bathtub and answered the door with no clothes on?" asked Cindy. "It was a guy selling vacuum cleaners. Talk about embarrassing!"

Karen giggled.

"That reminds me," Mrs. Brunner started to chuckle. "When Cindy was five years old—"

"Mom!" Cindy made a face. "You're not going to tell that story about the scissors, are you?"

"Not if you want to tell it," she answered.

Cindy groaned. "I gave myself a haircut. Big deal." She glared across the table at her mom. "For some reason, Mom thought it was hysterically funny."

Her mother leaned back in her chair. She sipped her diet cola and began to smile. "She cut two big hunks out of the side. She looked like a rooster when she was finished."

Tina laughed.

Mrs. Brunner stacked her plate on top of Karen's, carried the plates across the kitchen and dumped them in the trash compactor. "By the way," she said, turning, "I'm planning a party next weekend."

"What kind of party?" Cindy asked.

"A kind of celebration party," Mrs. Brunner said. "My exams are over and it looks like I'm going to get good grades in all my classes. Even that tough psychology class."

Cindy looked at Tina who was winking furiously at her. This must have something to do with the personal ad, Cindy thought. Tina sure was trying to get her attention.

"Tina, do you have something in your eye?" Mrs. Brunner asked with concern in her voice.

"No, Mrs. Brunner," Tina said innocently.

"Well, it will be nothing fancy," her mother continued. "Just a potluck barbeque with a few friends. I thought I'd ask everyone to bring a salad or a dessert. Maybe I'll ask Mr. Wattle to help me barbeque the chicken." Mrs. Brunner returned from the kitchen, wiping her hands on a dish towel. "Would you mind cleaning up the rest?" She tossed the towel over her shoulder and picked Karen up. "I want to give Karen a bath."

Karen stood on her seat, holding her arms out. "A bubble bath!"

"We'd be happy to help with the party, Mrs. Brunner," Tina said eagerly.

Too eagerly, Cindy thought. What was Tina up to?

Mrs. Brunner lifted Karen out of the booster chair and walked halfway to the bathroom. "Would you like to come to the barbeque?" she asked Tina. "To keep Cindy company?"

"That sounds like fun," Tina answered. "I'll ask Mom. Thanks!"

Cindy dropped her last piece of pizza half-eaten on her paper plate. She poked her straw at the crushed ice in the bottom of her glass, then slurped loudly. "The barbeque sounded like fun," she said, sadly, "until Mom mentioned Mr. Wattle. I think I'll spend the day locked in my room."

Tina began clearing the rest of the pizza mess

off of the table. "Stay in your room?" she asked, piling paper plates on top of each other. "Are you kidding? This is the break we've been waiting for!"

"Break? What do you mean?"

"We'll get the kind gentleman to come to the party," Tina said matter-of-factly. "Then, we'll keep Mr. Wattle occupied . . . " Tina slowed down at this point, as if she were just hatching a plan. "That won't be easy, but we'll figure something out. Then all we'll have to do is get your mom and the kind gentleman talking, and we're home free!"

"Hmmm. It might just work. If only we can find a way to get rid of Mr. Wattle . . . "

Tina's eyes grew big and round. "How about black dye in the barbeque sauce? That should keep Mr. Wattle busy," she said and both girls dissolved into giggles.

Suddenly, they were aware of someone standing in the doorway.

"What's so funny?" Mrs. Brunner asked.

Six

BY Monday morning, everything was going according to plan. Tina had contacted the paper Saturday morning so the invitation to the party would be in Monday's paper. Cindy and Tina had asked the kind gentleman to bring a pink bakery box filled with chocolate eclairs to the party so they'd know who he was. Tina had wanted him to wear a white carnation, but Cindy thought a bakery box would be less conspicuous at a cookout. She didn't know when she'd get around to telling her mother—if at all. Tina seemed to think it best to just let nature take its course. But it was hard to keep the whole thing a secret, especially when her mom was starting to notice how giggly the girls were acting.

Now Cindy had only two things to worry about—keeping Mr. Wattle occupied and making sure that she got the morning paper before her mother did.

She listened all morning for the newspaper to ka-plunk against their front door. Finally, she went out to the porch to look. *The Templeton Gazette* was sitting in the potted plant on the porch. That meant she'd missed seeing Paul this morning. It also meant that if she didn't hurry, she wouldn't make it to school in time for the meeting of the secret club. And Tina had said she had a great idea for initiation!

Cindy talked her mother into giving her a ride to school and arrived just five minutes before the bell and five minutes late to the meeting.

"Maybe we should have a rule about tardiness," Beth snapped at Cindy when Cindy entered the last stall.

"She's here, so what difference does it make?" Tina said. "Are you guys ready to hear my idea for the initiation?" she asked.

Cindy and Beth nodded eagerly.

"We're all going to Mrs. Brunner's barbeque." She raised an eyebrow at Beth and repeated, "*All* of us. Our job will be keeping Mr. Wattle occupied. That way, Mrs. Brunner will have time to chit-chat with the date we found her in the personal ads. That's the initiation for the club." She grinned widely. "Well, what do you think?"

Beth pulled a paper towel from the dispenser, twisting it nervously. "I think Mrs. Brunner's personal life is none of our business."

Cindy stared at her blankly. This was just like Beth!

"If you guys decide that's the initiation," Beth lowered her voice, "then I don't want any part of it."

Cindy watched Beth pick up her backpack and disappear through the door. "It isn't my fault my parents split up," Cindy called after her.

"Don't take it personally," Tina said. "She's just mad because we didn't pick crank telephone calls for our initiation. And because I got to be president first."

How could Cindy *not* take it personally? Her parents' divorce was a very personal matter.

* * * * *

Cindy thought about Beth's reaction for the rest of the day. She passed Tina a couple of notes about it, but Tina didn't seem too concerned. It would be up to the two of them, Tina said, to keep Mr. Wattle occupied. Beth would come around. She was just in a bad mood. But Cindy couldn't help but think she must have hurt Beth's feelings somehow. And that made Cindy feel just awful.

Things didn't get much better when Cindy got home from school. Her mom was sitting at the kitchen table squirting lo-cal sweetener into her coffee. All around her, cookbooks were spread open. She even had her recipe card file out which she hadn't used since the divorce.

"This is ridiculous!" Mrs. Brunner said as she slammed a cookbook closed. "There's no way I can make appetizers for twenty-five people. There aren't enough hours in the day."

"Twenty-five?" Cindy asked, setting her backpack on the table. "I thought this was going to be a simple barbeque."

"That was before I decided to invite my aerobics class," her mother said. "And what about the neighbors? Will their feelings be hurt if they're not invited?"

Cindy thought about old Mrs. Eldon with her houseful of cats and the Truscotts with their houseful of kids. "No," she said. "This should be an adult party. Except, of course, for me and Tina."

"Me, too!" Karen said, bounding into the room.

"You, too," Mrs. Brunner said, smiling. And then she frowned again. "Maybe I should just order cold cuts from the deli and forget about barbequing. My chicken always comes out burnt."

Cold cuts? Cindy thought. That meant baby beef tongue. Gross! She slid a cookbook across the table and turned to the chapter entitled, "Appetizers." There were recipes for everything from crisps to dips to canapes and spreads.

"Barbequed chicken is supposed to have a crispy skin," Cindy reassured her. "And what's the matter with chips and dip for an appetizer? It's not expensive and everyone likes to munch on chips and dip."

"Maybe we should forget the whole thing!" her mother said, sounding tired.

"You can't do that," Cindy said, a little too quickly. Her mother gave her a puzzled look. "I mean, think of all the people you'll be disappointing." Cindy said innocently.

"Yeah," her mother agreed. "Everyone I've talked to seemed to be looking forward to coming over."

"I'll tell you what," Cindy offered. "Tina and I will make the appetizers. Then you won't have anything to worry about, except the turkey—"

She stopped short. "I mean, the chicken."

Cindy grabbed the cookbook and went to call Tina. "We have to help Mom make an appetizer for the barbeque," she said.

"Appetizers?" Tina said. "We're going to have enough to do to keep Mr. Wattle occupied."

"But I *had* to volunteer," Cindy said. "Mom's really starting to get nervous about the party. She almost cancelled it." Cindy opened the cookbook and read from the appetizer table of contents. "This cookbook has recipes for kabobs, cocktail weiners, Hawaiian bites, marinated anchovies, miniature meatballs, and the usual dips and spreads."

"Read Hawaiian bites," Tina said. "And you'd better make it snappy before Mom finds out I'm on the phone."

"Are you grounded again?" Cindy asked.

"No," Tina answered. "Mom's just a little upset about how much time I spend on the phone. Hey, do you know what my little sister did last night when we were on the phone? She unraveled every roll of toilet paper in the house, the little monster. Too bad we don't know anyone who needs their house toilet papered. We'd be all set!"

Cindy giggled. "Okay, let's see. Hawaiian bites are on page forty-eight." She read, "Cut twenty canned water chestnuts in half; quarter ten chicken livers—"

"*Chicken livers?*" Tina snorted.

"You're right," Cindy agreed. "That's pretty disgusting. What about a cheeseball? There's a whole page on cheeseballs."

Tina didn't answer.

"Did you hear what I said?" Cindy repeated.

"Shhhh, I'm thinking!" Tina hushed. "That's it! I've got it!"

"What's *it*?"

"No, Mom," Tina shouted away from the receiver. "It's about homework. Listen, Cindy, I've got to go."

"You can't leave me hanging! What's *it*?"

"Okay, okay," Cindy heard Tina holler to her

mom. "I'm hanging up." Then she whispered to Cindy, "Wait'll you hear! You're gonna love it! No, Mom, we're talking about a history assignment. Cindy and I are—"

The receiver clicked and all Cindy heard was a dial tone.

Seven

CINDY woke up early the morning of the barbeque. Tina still hadn't told Cindy about her great idea. All Cindy knew was that it had something to do with a cheeseball. Cindy had made sure that her mother had all the ingredients on hand.

Tina arrived promptly at ten o'clock using the secret knock the two of them had developed for the club. Cindy scrambled to answer the door.

Tina carried a small overnight bag into the entrance hall of the Brunner's house.

Cindy eyed the suitcase. It was decorated with peeling bumper stickers. "What's in there?"

"My outfit for the barbeque."

"We'd better put it in my closet," Cindy said. "Mom'll have a fit if she thinks we're bringing junk *into* the house. She's emptied the trash ten times in the last two days and made half a dozen trips to Goodwill!"

"My mom's the same way before her parties," Tina agreed. "Doesn't it drive you crazy?"

Cindy put on her slippers and led the way to the kitchen. "Do you really think the *kind gentleman* will remember to bring chocolate eclairs to the barbeque?"

"In a pink bakery box," Tina added. "Of course he'll remember. That was the agreement."

"But what if he forgets? Then we won't know who he is."

Tina giggled. "We could always make it a party game. Find the missing man."

"Very funny," Cindy said nervously. "Now let's get started on that cheeseball. I'm dying to know what your great cheeseball idea is!"

"It's in my secret ingredient," Tina said opening the cookbook to the proper page. "First, we need one package of cream cheese." Tina's eyes had a mischievous gleam in them. "Then one jar of processed cheese spread, eight ounces of cheddar cheese, and one can of pitted olives." Cindy watched as Tina set everything on the counter. There didn't seem to be any secret ingredient there.

Then Tina unwrapped the cream cheese and plopped it into a bowl. "You grate the cheddar cheese. I'll work on the cream cheese. It says here to soften it," Tina said as she gave the cream cheese a hearty punch. "That's one way to soften it."

Cindy laughed and then began pleading with Tina. "Please, Tina. Come on. What's the secret ingredient?"

"In time, Cindy," Tina said, her eyes still gleaming.

Then Tina began reading the next step in the recipe. "Now it says to blend the cheeses with the mustard and worcester—whatever—it's called. Where's your electric mixer?"

"Over there," Cindy said, grating cheddar cheese. She scraped the cheese off the counter with a spatula and stuffed a measuring cup to the eight-ounce line. When everything was measured and poured, she said, "Okay. Let's plug in the electric mixer."

Tina plugged in the mixer and cheese flew all over the kitchen. "You're not supposed to plug it in when it's on *on!*" Cindy yelled.

"And you're not supposed to put the mixer in the bowl while I'm plugging it in!" Tina countered.

"Shhhhhh!" Cindy hushed. "I don't want Mom to hear us. She's been up since 5:30 dusting and cleaning." An orange glob of cheese slid down the front of the refrigerator. "I'll tell you one thing, you won't see me eating any of this stuff!"

Tina laughed, plopping to the floor. Orange polka dots of cheese were splattered across her face.

Cindy dropped to the floor next to Tina. The girls laughed until their sides ached and tears

rolled down their cheeks.

Karen surprised them from behind. "I'm telling!" she said loudly.

"Shhhhhh." Cindy put her finger to her mouth. "You don't want to ruin the surprise."

Karen fed her doll a piece of stray cheese. "Surprise?"

"We're making something for the party," Cindy whispered. "It's a surprise for Mom."

"Oh," Karen said. "I won't tell." She held her doll upside down by the foot and trotted down the hall.

Tina broke off a hunk of the cheese and formed two balls. "This is for the normal guests," she said pointing to one cheeseball. "And this one's for the turkey!" she said pointing to the other one.

"I don't get it," Cindy said.

Tina bent over and rolled up her pant leg. A bottle of tabasco sauce was sticking out of her sock. "This," Tina said, taking the bottle out of her sock, "is the secret ingredient. We're going to tell Mr. Wattle that your mom spent all day making the cheeseballs." She paused, pouring hot sauce over the cheese. "He'll have second thoughts about a permanent relationship when he finds out what a lousy cook she is. *And* it'll keep him out of the way through the whole party. He'll have to stay by the water faucet."

Cindy shook her head. "It'll never work."

"Sure it will. Because *we'll* be serving the cheese and crackers."

"I don't know," Cindy said, skeptically.

"Mr. Wattle can't say anything about the cheeseballs," Tina went on, "He wouldn't dare tell your mom she's a lousy cook."

"Who's a lousy cook?" Mrs. Brunner asked. She stood in the doorway that connected the garage to the kitchen. Her hair was tied up in a red bandana and her cheeks were smudged with dirt. Dirty rags were draped over her shoulder.

Cindy quickly stepped in front of the cheeseballs. "Lousy cook?" she asked innocently. "I don't know any lousy cooks. Do you, Tina?"

Tina was wrapping the cheeseballs in foil. "Not me," she said, crinkling foil.

"Is there anything else we can do to help?" Cindy asked.

Mrs. Brunner picked at a piece of cheese that had dried on the oven door. Then she pulled a list from her pocket. "Would you mind hosing off the patio?" Then Mrs. Brunner looked around at the cheese splattered kitchen. "And cleaning the kitchen?"

The girls nodded.

It was twelve-thirty by the time they'd finished sweeping and hosing the patio. The guests were due to arrive at two o'clock. The kind gentleman was supposed to arrive an hour later. That way, Tina and Cindy would be sure to notice him.

Cindy opened her closet door and flipped through the hangers. "I guess it's jeans and a T-shirt." Her favorite T-shirt read, *Golf is a ball— no matter which way you slice it.* It was her favorite because the bottom was long enough to tie in a big knot. Besides, it used to belong to her dad, and it made her feel good to wear it.

Tina lifted her suitcase to the bed. She held up her T-shirt, *Grandma went to Hawaii and all I got was this lousy T-shirt!*

The girls wore the same jeans they always wore on weekends. Thread-thin at the knees. Cindy opened the drawer filled with her mom's used makeup. She was brushing her cheeks with a frosted blushing powder when there was a knock at Cindy's door. "What is it?" Cindy called.

"Telephone," her mom answered.

Cindy raced down the hall, hoping Paul was on the phone.

"Hi," Beth said. "Would you like to go to the movies this afternoon?"

Cindy was surprised. "Me?"

"Is this Cindy?"

Cindy nodded. "Yeah, but aren't you still mad?"

"Just because I quit the club doesn't mean I'm mad at you."

"Then why don't you eat lunch with Tina and

me anymore?" Cindy asked.

"I got tired of listening to you guys talk about your divorced parents," Beth said. "Who they're dating. What kinds of cars they drive. What they do for a living. Whether or not they're parent material—"

"It's not my fault my parents split up," Cindy interrupted.

"No one's blaming you," Beth went on. "But that's all you guys talk about. It's s-o-o-o-o boring!"

"Who's supposed to take care of Mom? Now that Dad's not around?"

"See what I mean? We can't even have a conversation on the phone without your parents coming into it."

Cindy sighed loudly. "Sometimes I wish I could get Mom and her dates off my mind. Sometimes, I want to forget the whole thing!"

"Don't you think she's old enough to make her own decisions about dating?" Beth asked.

"I used to think so," Cindy said, "until she

started dating Mr. Wattle. Now I don't know."

"Well, the whole thing scares me," Beth said.

"Scares you? Why?" Cindy asked.

"Well," Beth began slowly. "I mean, if your parents got divorced, mine could, too. I mean, they have these stupid arguments and don't talk to each other for an hour and . . ." Beth stopped to catch her breath. "Well, maybe that's why I don't like to talk about divorce."

Cindy understood what Beth was saying. It must be hard for Beth to be the only member of the club whose parents were still together. It probably makes her worry all the time about her own parents.

"Your parents aren't going to get divorced," Cindy said reassuringly. "And even if they do, it's not so bad. You can adjust." Cindy paused for a second. She half-believed what she was telling Beth. "Take my house, for instance," she said. "Things are going to be a lot different around here after today."

"Really?" Beth asked. "What's happening

today? What's going to change?"

It made Cindy dizzy to think about the many things on the day's agenda. Mr. Wattle, the hot sauce cheeseball, the man with the pink bakery box . . . .

Then Tina stepped in the doorway. "Guess what briefcase-carrying nerd-ball is at your front door collecting for the newspaper?"

Eight

CINDY opened the front door and stepped onto the porch. "Hi," she said to Paul. "How much do we owe?"

A pair of roller skates were knotted and hanging over Paul's shoulder. "Owe?" he asked with a puzzled tone in his voice. "Oh, for the newspaper. I'm not really making my collection rounds. I just said that to Tina because I didn't know what else to say. It took me off guard when she answered the door."

Cindy didn't know what to say either. If Paul wasn't collecting for the newspaper, then why was he there? She certainly couldn't ask him a question like that—not to his face!

"I was just wondering," Paul began. "If you'd like to go roller skating?"

"Roller skating? *Me*?"

"If you're not doing anything," he said, shyly. "But I guess you're busy, huh? Since Tina's here. I've got a pocketful of quarters I've been wanting to get rid of—you know how heavy a pocketful of quarters is."

Cindy nodded. "Yeah."

"So it wouldn't cost you anything."

Cindy couldn't believe what was happening. Paul McCloskey was asking her out on a date! A real live date—where the guy pays and everything!

"Mom's having this barbeque," she said sadly. "And I sort of promised to help out."

"Yeah." Paul nodded shyly. "I guess it was short notice."

"Maybe we could go skating some day after school," Cindy suggested. "I mean—if you still want to."

"How about Monday?" Paul asked eagerly.

"We could ride our bikes."

"Monday would be great!"

Paul bounced down the front steps and picked his bike up off the lawn. He swung a leg over the seat and turned toward Cindy. "See you," he said.

"Yeah, see you."

The front door opened and Cindy fell backward into the living room. "What did he want anyway?" Tina demanded. "I didn't see you give him any money for the newspaper."

"You were eavesdropping!"

"No I wasn't," she said, closing the door. "I was peeking through the curtains."

"You know what?" Cindy asked. "I don't even care if you were eavesdropping or if you call Paul a dumb name. Because *he* asked *me* for a date."

Tina was impressed. "A date? Really? Where he pays and everything?"

Cindy nodded happily. "Yup."

"Gee. That's really neat, Cindy," Tina said. "No one has ever asked me to do anything unless

I paid. Maybe Paul's not such a geek after all."

Two hours later, the Brunner living room was filled with guests. Cindy tried to keep an eye on the time. The serving of the cheeseballs had to be perfectly timed for right before the kind gentleman arrived.

Cindy was trying to act casual when she felt a tap on her head. "Don't you girls look cute," Mr. Wattle said.

"Thank you," Cindy said, ducking his hand pat. "I'd like you to meet my friend, Tina. Tina, this is Mr. Wattle."

Tina extended her hand. "I've been looking forward to this."

"What a wonderful party," Mr. Wattle said, making casual conversation. "Everyone seems to be having a good time."

"It would've been better," Tina said, "if the caterers hadn't quit."

"Caterers?" Mr. Wattle questioned.

"*Caterers?*" Cindy repeated.

"Yeah, caterers," Tina continued, grinning

gleefully. "The check for the deposit Mrs. Brunner gave them bounced."

"Excuse us," Cindy said. She grabbed Tina by the arm. "We have to help in the kitchen."

The girls zigzagged around the guests. "How could you say something so stupid?" Cindy shrieked. "What if he says something about the caterers to Mom?"

"He won't," Tina said confidently. "The last thing he would want to do is embarrass her."

Cindy glanced at her wristwatch. "It's time," she said. Tina opened a box of sesame seed crackers and arranged them on two platters. Then Cindy got the cheeseballs—with and without the hot sauce—out of the refrigerator. She glanced at the crowd. Everyone was busy sipping punch and sinking vegetables into dip. Mrs. Brunner was bustling from one person to another. No one, thank goodness, was paying attention to what was going on in the kitchen.

Cindy saw Mr. Wattle through the kitchen window. He poured the charcoal into the barbeque pit, and squirted it with lighter fluid.

"Daddy never uses lighter fluid," she said, sadly. "It gives the food a funny taste."

"Maybe now would be a good time to offer Mr. Wattle cheese and crackers," Tina suggested. "Since he's by himself."

Cindy fidgeted nervously. "I don't know."

Everything was happening so fast. *Too fast.* There wasn't enough time to think things out. That didn't seem to bother Tina. She acted first and thought later, if she bothered to think at all.

Cindy glanced at the clock on the stove. She expected the man with the chocolate eclairs in fifteen minutes. "I guess it's now or never," she said.

She picked up the platter with the spicy cheeseball and slipped through the sliding glass door. Mr. Wattle was building a mountain of coals in the center of the barbeque. He wiped his hands on his apron, smudging it black. That's when Cindy noticed the apron Mr. Wattle was wearing had belonged to her dad.

Cindy held up the tray. "Would you like some-thing to snack on?"

Mr. Wattle spread cheese across a cracker. "Thank you, Cindy."

"Take two," she said. "They're small."

Mr. Wattle spread a second cracker, took a napkin, and set them down next to his iced tea. "Thanks, again."

Karen squeezed through the back door. She was cradling her doll. And she was feeding it the empty bottle of tabasco sauce.

"Take that back in the house!" Cindy ordered.

Karen stuck out her tongue. The bottle slipped from her fingers and rolled across the patio. It didn't stop until it hit Mr. Wattle's brown oxfords.

"What's this?" he asked, picking up the bottle.

Karen ran to Mr. Wattle and she tugged on his pant leg. "Give me my catsup!" she demanded. "It's mine!"

Cindy, meanwhile, had made a backward exit into the house. She huddled next to Tina in the

kitchen. They watched wide-eyed through the window.

Mr. Wattle lifted Karen up to his hip. "You don't want that dirty old thing," he said, setting the bottle down. Then he gave her a tabasco-covered cracker instead.

"He's going to kill her!" Cindy gasped.

Karen took the cracker and sniffed the cheese. Then she grabbed the second cracker and made a tabasco sandwich. "Ummmmmmm," she said, holding it up to her doll's mouth.

The she offered the cracker to Mr. Wattle. He opened his mouth for a nibble, she shoved the whole thing in—crackers, cheese, tabasco, and all!

"Now *she's* killing *him!*" Cindy groaned. "He wasn't supposed to eat both of them! Not at the same time!"

Mr. Wattle's eyeballs grew until they looked as though they'd pop out of his head. His nose twitched and his lower lip puckered. He ran into the house and pushed through the crowd, making his way to the bathroom.

The girls followed him down the hall. They pressed their ears against the closed bathroom door. The sound coming from inside was a mixture of coughing and wheezing.

"Thank goodness," Cindy said. "At least he's alive." It was time to remove herself from the scene of the crime. Her bedroom wasn't the safest place. But it was the only place. "Do you think the other guests know what happened?"

Cindy leaned against her bedroom door and imagined everyone buzzing with the news of Mr. Wattle's poisoning. It would probably make the headlines in tomorrow's newspaper: *Man poisoned at Mrs. Brunner's barbeque.*

"Wow!" Tina said, looking out the window. "Look at the car that just pulled into the driveway. Do you know how much a car like that costs? You'd have to be a zillionaire to afford it! You don't suppose . . . hey, Cindy! It's the guy with the pink bakery box."

Cindy rushed to the window. "Oh, brother,"

she said. "I almost forgot about him!"

"Look at what he's wearing! What a hunk!" She turned to Cindy. "If it turns out your Mom doesn't like this guy, can I have him for my mom?"

Then another car pulled up in the driveway. "It's Nana!" Cindy said, surprised. "I didn't know she was driving up from Los Angeles." She pressed her nose against the glass. "Oh, my gosh. *Look*! She's talking to the man with the bakery box!"

The two girls watched Nana and the man with the bakery box walk up the driveway. "What a lucky break!" Tina said. "Now your mom will think he came with your Nana. Isn't that perfect?"

No, Cindy didn't think it was perfect. She wished April on her soap opera had never placed a personal ad. And that she'd never placed the personal ad for her mom.

"Come on, we'd better get back to the party," Tina said, dragging Cindy by the arm.

The girls squatted behind a bushy fern. "There they are," Cindy whispered. "Nana and the man with the bakery box are *both* talking to Mom! I can't take this—I'm packing my bags and heading for the bus station."

"Why? This is great!" Tina whispered back. "Look, your mom's even laughing! Can you believe it?!"

Cindy watched her mom and the man with the pink bakery box. No, she couldn't believe it. How could her mom be having fun with someone she just met? She suddenly felt a tightness in her throat. It was the same feeling she had the night her mom kissed Mr. Wattle on the cheek.

"They're acting like old friends," Tina said. "Didn't I tell you I knew what I was doing?"

Cindy moaned. "I've seen enough."

Tina followed Cindy into her bedroom. "What's wrong with you, Cindy? *Everything* is going the way we planned it. So what's the problem?"

Cindy took her favorite position, backward, on

her bed. She wrapped her arms tightly around her pillow. "I don't know what's wrong," she said, miserably. "Normally I would've run up to Nana and given her a big hug and a kiss. But I couldn't even do that, not with that man standing there. *Everything's* wrong. That's what's wrong."

A knock on the door startled the girls. It opened and Mrs. Brunner peeked in the room. "May I come in?" she asked with a serious look on her face.

Cindy sat up quickly. "I guess so. I mean, sure."

Tina was busily tossing her clothes and makeup into her suitcase. She snapped the latches and lifted it by the handle. "It's been a nice party, Mrs. Brunner. But I have to be going."

Cindy glared at her friend. "You're in this as much as I am."

"I want to talk to *both of you*," Mrs. Brunner added pointedly.

Tina dropped to the edge of the bed, sitting next to Cindy. "Well, I guess we've had it now," she said under her breath.

"To begin with," Mrs. Brunner said, "I'd like an explanation of *this*." She tossed a section of the newspaper on the bed. It was folded to the classified ads section. The personal ad column was circled with a red marker.

Cindy stared blankly at the paper. "I was only trying to help."

"Help? *Help* with what?" her mom asked. "What would make you do such a thing?"

"I didn't want Mr. Wattle as a stepfather," Cindy said sadly. "I thought if I placed an ad I could get someone just right. But I guess it didn't work, did it?"

Mrs. Brunner took a deep breath and exhaled loudly. She tried to regain her composure. "Of course it didn't work," she said. "Have you stopped to think what might've happened if I didn't know Dr. Simmons?"

The girls exchanged glances. "Dr. Simmons?"

"The man who answered the ad," Mrs. Brunner explained. "He's my psychology professor. But

what if I didn't know him? That would make him a stranger, wouldn't it? Cindy, how many times have I told you not to talk to strangers? And what do you do? You invite a perfect stranger into our house!"

"I didn't think about him being a stranger," Cindy said.

"Me either," Tina added.

"Did you *know* the person who answered the ad?" Cindy's mother asked.

The girls shook their heads.

"*That's* the definition of a stranger."

"And Cindy, there are other reasons that what you did is wrong. It's more than just inviting strangers into our house."

Cindy sighed and looked at Tina. The two of them prepared themselves for a long lecture.

"Cindy," her mother started, sounding a little tired. "This divorce has been tough on everyone. It's been hard on you and Karen. But it's also been hard on me. I'm going to be dating men other than your father. That's just the way it's going to be. And I need to do it on my own, without the two of you interfering."

Cindy nodded, but she really didn't understand.

"Look, Cindy," her mother said. "What if I set up a date for you to go bowling with the son of one of the women from my aerobics class? What would you think of that?"

Cindy thought about it. She wouldn't like it, especially now that Paul had finally asked her on a real date. Maybe that's how her mom was feeling about the personal ad and Mr. Wattle.

Before Cindy had a chance to answer, her grandmother peeked in the room. "Is this a private party?" Cindy's grandmother asked. "Or can anyone join?"

"Nana," Cindy squealed. She jumped up from the bed and threw her arms around her grandmother's waist. "I'm so glad you're here! But why didn't you tell us that you were coming?"

"I thought I'd keep my trip a surprise," she said, returning the hug. "But judging from what's been going on around here, you have more than enough surprises."

"We're having a little talk about dating, Mom," Mrs. Brunner said, smiling for the first time at Cindy and Tina. "I'm trying to make Cindy understand that it wasn't Mr. Wattle she didn't like. She'd probably feel the same way about any man I dated."

Cindy thought for a moment. "I think I know what you mean, Mom," she said. "I wasn't any happier when I saw you talking to the man with the box than I was when I saw you with Mr. Wattle. It just doesn't feel right unless it's Daddy."

"And Mr. Wattle really isn't a turkey," Cindy's grandmother said. "You'd think any man your mom dated was a turkey. Because that would mean that she and your dad wouldn't be getting back together."

Cindy's mom ruffled Cindy's hair. "Cindy, I know you feel bad. I know it hurts to miss Dad. And I know it's going to be hard for you to see me dating other men. But you have to trust me. It'll get easier."

"She's right," Tina agreed. "It doesn't bother me when my mom goes out anymore—at least not as much as it used to."

"It's okay to feel bad, Cindy," her grandmother said. "What's not okay is to interfere."

Cindy nodded at her grandmother and her mother. Then she gave Tina a weak smile. This divorce stuff was tough. But Tina was probably right. It would get easier.

"There's one last thing that I have to talk with you about," Cindy's mom said.

Cindy knew what was coming—Mr. Wattle and the cheeseball.

"Mr. Wattle has been very understanding about your little prank," she went on. "And he has something he wants to ask you."

"Ask *me*?" Cindy whined. "Do I have to?"

Mrs. Brunner kissed the top of her daughter's head. "You *and* Tina have to."

"Ugh!" Cindy said. "Here goes nothing."

Nana winked. "I'm pulling for you sport."

Cindy smiled. "Thanks."

Mr. Wattle was standing in the living room next to the potted palm. His eyes had gone back into their sockets and his lower lip had lost its pucker. "Ah-ha," he said. "If it isn't the hot sauce kids."

Cindy and Tina exchanged looks. "I'm sorry about the cheeseball," she said. *"Really sorry."*

"Me, too," Tina said.

"Mom said you had something you wanted to ask us?"

Mr. Wattle nodded. "Yes, I do."

Cindy was ready to accept her punishment, whatever it was.

"Since you two are so creative in the kitchen," Mr. Wattle said. "Would you mind helping me barbeque the chicken?"

Cindy was taken by surprise. *"That's* what you wanted to ask us?"

Mr. Wattle smiled. "Is it a deal?" he asked.

The girls exchanged looks and giggled. "It's a deal!"

About the Author

SHERRY SHAHAN is married and has two daughters. She and her family live on a horse ranch called Hidden Oaks in California where they breed and raise racehorses. Sherry considers herself an "adventurer at heart." Every year, she and her husband take a special trip to a foreign land and explore the countryside on horseback. They have traveled across Argentina, Kenya, New Zealand, and Hawaii on horses.

Sherry has been a writer for ten years. She gets her inspiration from everyday life with her own children. She also writes articles for magazines about her travels.

When Sherry is not busy writing or chauffeuring her children, she enjoys aerobics, jogging, and bicycling.